D1551379

WHERE I STAY

To all those I've lied to.

Aug. 2, Cheyenne, Wyoming

Perpendicular to the road and sagging between the outstretched arms of crossed wood crutches are several irrigation pipes leaking water. As far as the eye can see are gold, spent fields of grain, cut only by the pencil-thin shadows of the irrigators and the hulking aluminum and plexiglass canopy of the thresher, lying in wait between the rows. There are birds, and silver ribbons tied in the crops to scare the birds away. A tractor drives by, the driver waving one arm in salute, the hot diesel fumes puttering out in short bursts behind the man-high tires. There is a house in the distance, neighbored by a silo and a satellite dish winking reflectively in the sun. A car hurtles down the road, bringing bleached white Utah plates and a trio of kids gawking through the back window, their mouths tiny O's pressed against the glass. They pass in a blur, a rush of wind. A moment later there is a sound from the fields. The crops move, a white hat bobs in and out of the golden sea. A thin girl with pig-tails pouring out from under the brim of her fisherman's cap pops out from the field. She looks straight ahead, sticks out her stomach and puts one hand in her jeans. Her other hand is full of stones. Her bare feet are covered with streaks of dirt and her face is red from sun. The tip of her nose bends upward slightly and she looks at the horizon without really looking. Then just as suddenly, she's off, kicking at a space in the mud near the toothed wheel that turns the big irrigators, digging at the mud with her toes. *What are you doing?* She stops and stares. Picking rocks, she says. Flicking her toes upwards she uproots a stone and it glimmers in the dirt like a tortoise shell. She puts it in her hand, turns, disappears.

of the workers detaches himself from the group. Skin darkened by sun and tar, his mustache seems painted on his face, his elbows poke out strangely, his hands stay tucked into the belly of his overalls. Hello, Tom, he says. Tom the driver raises two fingers. The mustached worker peers into the cab. You getting on alright, Tom? A walkie-talkie squawks. Tom opens his mouth. The woman steps backwards and begins waving her flags. The engine of the big rig behind the pickup rattles out of idle. Tom is about to speak. Tom hesitates. A car back in the line honks. And honks again. Tom leans forward, shakes his head, slaps the car into gear, puts his foot on the gas and passes on through, onto the open lane. In unison, the empty faces of the workers turn to stare. The woman keeps waving her flags. Tom twists his hand against the wheel. He knocks his knuckles against the windshield. He rubs his knuckles into his forehead. He rolls down the window and opens a second beer. His hands move over the radio dial and the mountains begin to slide by again. Well, I can still go fishing and they can't, Tom says.

This is Tom.

Aug. 7, Rt. 93, Nevada

Flat, shorn earth—broken only by the road. Northbound, cars pass. When there are no cars, the sun, the road, the earth, and a lone shadow are all there is. The air-brakes of a truck hiss and release. The driver opens the truck door. He speaks in long sentences, drawn-out American words mixed with quickly stuttered Spanish. His mouth moves with rapid flashes of bent and discolored teeth. When a car with girls in it passes by, he honks his horn while looking down at their legs. From high up in the cab all you can see is their legs. Dinner is in a booth reserved for drivers only at a casino truck stop in Nevada. At another truck stop outside Reno we stop for the night. Outside, the trucks grumble as they sleep. It is a gypsy city . . . gypsies riding on the backs of giant, rumbling monsters. Dust shrouded pictures and words are drawn in the dirt that encases the trailers. In the top bunk of the cab, the breath of the air conditioner roars as loud as the ocean.

I tied guitar strings around my wrists, around my ankles. I pierced my ears, my nose with a needle. I put guitar strings in the holes. I stood in front of a truck stop bathroom mirror and used pliers to twine the ends together. The ends were sharp, I had marks across my forearms from where they tore at the skin, they pulled at the fabric of my clothes.

Aug. 12, Los Angeles, California

The officer at the door of the Greyhound bus terminal will not let people in without a ticket. So, it's outside where two black men are resting and talking. One is older and shorter, with wiry stubble covering his face. The other, his skin is smooth, and on one arm a medical patch covers a vein in the crook of his arm. The older man talks about New York. He says that in that city you cannot walk down a street with your woman because if you do someone will point a gun to your head. *Yes, New York is no good.* Heads nod. The younger man asks if I can go inside and get him a cup of water. The glass door opens, the guard steps forward. *I just need a bus schedule.* The guard holds open the door. At the small food stand inside, if you pay a nickel, they give you a cup filled with water. Outside I hand the water to the young man who gulps it down. He pauses for an instant and then spits it all out. That's warm water goddammit! He clutches his stomach. He throws the styrofoam cup. The older man flashes his teeth. That's all right, he says, don't worry. A few minutes later everyone is asleep. A pimp wades through the sleepers. He pokes me and prods at my ribcage. *What?* I doesn't know English, the pimp says, pointing at a hotel advertisement in a telephone book. He asks the address of the hotel. The address is crossed out. The name and number of a woman are scrawled across the page. Eventually he looks up, he stares into the face he is looking at. After a moment he slams the telephone book closed and walks away. The last thing I see is his baggy neon pants, striped yellow and black, clinging slightly to the front of his thighs as he turns the corner.

Aug. 17, Tijuana, Mexico

Lying in the arms of a man, who says his name, as an unfamiliar ceiling stares down at the bed. *Where are we?* Tijuana, he says. He miscounted some money. This is the second time he has been fired in ten days. Last time was from a dance club, Bottoms Up!, when someone tore one of his dresses and he went crazy, ripping all the dancer's costumes into ribbons. Bitches! he cried then, Faggot-Bitches! Today, we spend all day in bed trying to teach me Spanish. He pronounces the words slowly, his lips traced with my finger. A delivery man comes, we eat Chinese food from containers propped up between the pillows. Later that night, there is some crying and a dream. The dream is that these two men are connected with several aluminum umbilical cords. The cords grow tighter and pull them closer together. They begin to make love. When they are about to finish one pulls away because suddenly he is aware that one of them will strangle the other.

In my bag I carried a comic book, black cover: The Death of Superman. I thought if I had to I could always sell it. Eventually I used the cardboard backing to sit on when it was raining.

Aug. 19, Mexicali, Mexico

. . . rusted black Chevy with spots of grey primer dotting its side. A lean, tan forearm dangles outside the window. It holds up one outstretched palm and four fingers, the index finger missing, the middle one taped over the knuckle with adhesive. You got cigarettes? *Yes.* Well now, jump in cabron. The car hisses and jerks to the ground, dipping to the pavement. Then the pneumatics rise, pushing our tongues between our teeth. The two men, twins, howl and beat their hands against the dashboard. One has a radio in his lap. He nods his head at the thumping bass. He turns and grins as he is handed a pair of cigarettes. He tears the filter off his own and sticks what's left between his teeth. The driver picks the filtered cigarette out of the palm of his brother. The two men unroll their windows and wind swirls into the back seat. They finish their cigarettes and then the one in the passenger seat puts a soda can between his knees and methodically perforates it with a fork. From a plastic baggy he pulls out several brown gummy threads, spreads the threads across the holes in the can and lights them. Sucking smoke into his mouth, he exhales through his nostrils, tears coming to his eyes. He passes the can to the back seat. Red strings of capillaries hold his pupils in place as his lips spread wide. Speak Spaneesh? he says, wiping his eyes with the back of his hand. His teeth span from cheek to cheek. *No.* Too bad cabron, he says laughing. That's too bad.

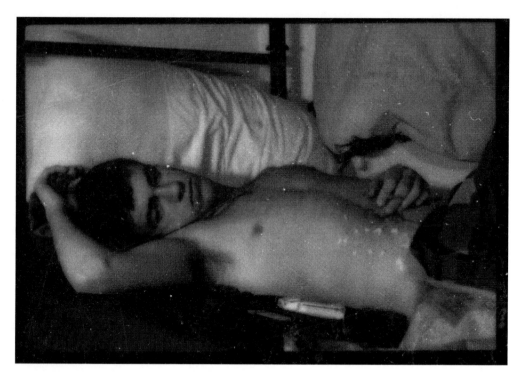

I have systematically and selectively removed myself from my past. The past does not fit in my present tense.
I do not fit in myself.

At times I felt that these two were my real parents.

Aug. 27, Mexico City, Mexico

In the afternoon, it rains. A ring of mountains around the city traps all the pollution. With my fingers bunched in my palm, I can rub a raindrop until only grit remains. On the benches, in the shadow of a statue of Christopher Columbus, in a square across the American embassy, a group of prostitutes congregates on the benches, new members strolling in as other ones speed away in the tiny white taxis that buzz by all night. Sometimes they come out of the taxis bringing food, other times they bring cigarettes. They are often bored. I teach them how to play gin and they play all night long, someone taking another's hand when work appears. Soon they have learned well enough that they beat me easily. Their dark eyes reveal nothing, except when they are laughing or being threatened. The youngest, and darkest boy, brings in brown-tar heroin and behind the bushes the boys shoot up. The boys laugh because their new member is afraid of needles and has broken the point off one so he can shoot the tar up his nose. During the day the syringes and the empty bottles that litter the ground are swept away. Where the new one sleeps, the area is clear and the dirt is darker, imprinted with the weight of his body on a blanket. The boys skirt around it cautiously, careful, for some reason, not to step within that rectangle.

In June of 1982 my sister tried to kill herself. She came to me and said, "There are no sheets, the pillows are full of glass." She had a bottle of aspirin in one hand and lithium in the other. The telephone rang and when I returned she was gone. A trail of blood dotted the wooden floor, there was a steak knife with its point propped up against the porch door. In the bathroom, my mother bound her forearms with masking tape. On the ride to the hospital my sister opened the car window and battered her neck against the top edge of it and then tried to jump out of the car and then stuck her fist down her throat.

Aug. 9, Sacramento, California

The strong summer heat reflects off the aluminum warehouse walls and hangs like a cloud above the towers of storage shelves. It's my job just to do the driving, says Jose. I'll note that, says the clerk, rolling a large hydraulic cart along the floor. Jose unloads box after box of soap dishes and tennis rackets. If you hadn't come on Sunday, we wouldn't have this problem and I wouldn't have to be here, says the clerk. I'll note that, says Jose. Time passes. The truck leaves the warehouse, lighter but not running any faster, dredging the long tunnel of the central valley. Fourteen hours later, the cab door opens outside San Dimas. I will see you again, Jose says. He points to the gray-blue sky and then past it, beyond the white, melon sun. A cross dangles from his chest. I will see you up *there*.

Aug. 4, Dubois, Wyoming

The dawn air is cool, but it won't stay that way and walking backwards the town recedes and the cars surge forward. Dust and wind blow off the butte and onto the highway. The drivers stare at the horizon without really looking or point off the road to show they aren't going far. A pick-up stops, the passenger door pushed open, and then the land begins moving, moving much faster now, until finally civilization is gone and the truck is between places. The cab of the truck bounces, a fisherman's fly hangs on a rod stuck through the cab and the fly's little feathers twitch as it swivels on the line. Left the kids behind, says the driver. He points to the back. There's some beer in the load and he asks for it. The ring tabs pop. Lost my fucking J-O-B, he says. Third project this month. No backhoe. It's just a few miles now and you'll get to see it. Sons of shittin' bitches. Outside, the mountains slide by. The driver downshifts up the grade. Well, now I'm just going fishing now, he says. *Just going fishing now.* All righty, he says. You're all right. The forest creeps down to the highway. Ahead is a traffic cone and a woman in shorts, her legs straddle the yellow divider, her hands wave two orange flags. The man takes his foot off the gas. Stick with me now, he says, stick with me. Three Caterpillar steam rollers, each the size of a small building and each belching billowing clouds of black smoke, vibrate in wait alongside a jagged pile of pavement ripped from the road. The pick-up stops and the acrid smell of hot asphalt pours in as the driver unrolls his window. The woman wears thick, goggle-like sunglasses and her hair tucked back under her cap. She rests the white plastic butt of one flag against her hip. You new? Just started on Monday, she says. She pulls down her glasses and winks. The man nods and fingers the blinker switch. You're doing just fine then, he says. A group of men sit in front of a trailer off the shoulder and the man driving keeps looking out at them. They look away. Just fine then, the driver says. Eventually one

I want you to know how it was with me.

"These anonymous people who come and go in the cities and who move on the land; it is on what they look like, now; what is in their faces and in the windows and the streets beside and around them; what they are wearing and what they are riding in, and how they are gesturing, that we need to concentrate, consciously, with the camera."

—Walker Evans, 1938

WHERE I STAY
ANDREW ZORNOZA

TS PRESS
2009

Andrew Zornoza, Where I Stay
© 2009 Andrew Zornoza

First edition, May 2009
ISBN: 9780977901913
Printed and bound in the USA
Library of Congress Control Number: 2009926988

Cover photo by Bryan Schutmaat (www.bryanschutmaat.com)
Cover & book design by Christian Peet
Text is in Garamond, titles in Nimbus Sans Novus

Tarpaulin Sky Press
PO Box 189
Grafton, Vermont 05146
www.tarpaulinsky.com

For more information on Tarpaulin Sky Press perfect-bound and hand-bound editions, as well as information regarding distribution, personal orders, and catalogue requests, please visit our website at www.tarpaulinsky.com.

In Mexico I had diarrhea all the time. One day we went out to see the temples outside of town. On the way back we stopped at a monastery and I squatted amidst the ruins of an old foundation. I was proud that I had lost all ability to be self conscious. When I was done one of the prostitutes punched me in the groin, "You should not be so proud," he said. "It is not good to be nothing."

Sept. 3 & 4, Matamoros, Mexico & Brownsville, Texas

Midnight at the U.S./Mexican border. The Rio Grande is anemic, dull—a muddy moat under the moon and halogen lights. There is a convenience store, a gas station, a fruit stand, and a wide flat plain dotted with plots of scrubby forest. Searchlights scan the horizon. . . . A helicopter. A radio blares in Spanish voices. A wooded area a hundred feet behind the convenience store . . . there is no place to hide, no underbrush, only the emaciated trunks of cypress. You can't hear yourself move. The helicopter sends waves of sound through the air. I can't hear myself. I hold a small trinket from Eva that is a temple to Guadeloupe, the patron saint of Mexico. It is formed in the style of a miniature wallet, when you undo the snap it unfolds in four panels. On the panels are pictures of the infant Jesus, pictures of Guadeloupe, a Bible verse, and a small medallion. But it is still full of scent: soap, smoke, and perfume. I attach it onto a necklace of string. There is no sleep, just fear and waiting. There is the smell of Eva, crowded between my face and the mesquite. Finally a dim light from the east, two immigration officers kicking and cussing through the woods. Cupped fingers in rubber gloves push my testicles, probe the edges of my asshole. The two men pull away in their jeep. The sun rises. Down the road, at the overpass, an old-timer crouched in the posture of a soldier flings grass at oncoming cars with one hand. His other hand covers a bible tucked under his arm like a football. A beat-up suit clings desperately to his shoulders. He gestures to a concrete drainage tunnel below us. We can sleep there, he says. He pushes a book of psalms into the sky and gestures at the retreating shadows. There are snakes in the desert!

There was heat and barbed wire, train tracks in the distance. I had walked too far down the road, there were no cars, I had no water, no food. I woke up and I was beating my face into the sand. On the opposite side of the road was a test bombing ground for the US military. Two fighter jets screamed past overhead. I remember that I crawled back to the truck stop, I gave up going south but really I did not know what I was doing. On the westbound ramp, Jose stopped for me. He showed

me a picture of his nephew. He gave me a road atlas that I could fit in my back pocket. Later, I opened it and found the road where I had been, Rt. 93. I drew tiny little X's along it, I marked it as a place I never wanted to return to. But I would return, many times.

Sept. 9, Odessa, Texas

A truck-stop . . . a diner . . . a busboy. The busboy asks his sister if they have room at their place. Their grandmother crouches in a corner and rolls tortillas with the palms of her veined hands. She stuffs the tortillas with seared beef and pimientos. The boy's name is Omar and his father makes crosses out of string and pipe cleaners to make cigarette money while he is in prison. Omar has hundreds of these little crosses and now both of us are wearing them. We smoke a lot of pot together. It is so cold that we cut the bottoms off the legs of a pair of sweat pants and wear them as hats. I smoke a lot of weed but Omar smokes a lot more. The grandmother comes into the room and in broken English says that with the marijuana her grandson is like a fat man who hasn't eaten. Omar then tells me that sometimes he carves marijuana leaves in the glass panes of kids' car windows for money. The next morning he drives me down to Rt. 10. Cars are swerving off the road, honking their horns, flying by at hundreds of miles per hour. We are on the wrong side of the highway and Omar flips the wheel and sends the car onto the grassy divider. Laughter—happiness.

Aug. 23, Yuma, Arizona

The trucks huddle together like covered wagons, there is only one car. The car is a Pontiac, a V-8, the trunk is longer than the hood. The hood rumbles, heat shimmering at its borders. Pots and pans crash in the back seat like cymbals. Lonnie's long fingers roll the cigarette paper and with a collapsing figure eight deftly tuck it into a tube. Strands of tobacco stick to her thumbs. She has a thick, broken nose and looks like a man. Lonnie and her husband stop at each town and Lonnie goes to the police station. We're outta gas, she tells them. Her husband's hat is cocked off his head at an angle, a feather droops from his ear. Charity is the law down here, he says to me. A thorny rose tattoo bends across the plates of his chest. He picks the knife right out of my hip pocket, unfolds the blade with one finger and passes it back while his other hand steadies the wheel. This might be good, he says, winking, for killing rabbits.

I was at Niagara Falls with my sister. Strings of white foam ran through the water like pulled taffy. Purple neon lights illuminated the cliffs only to die in darkness at the river bottom.

"Can we get closer?" she shouted.

"The road turns ahead," I said. "This is as far as we go."

I pulled my jacket tight around my shoulders and tucked my chin into my neck for warmth. Rising out of the opposite bank,

like a maypole, was a towering cylinder of light. A dozen or more cascading ribbons of shifting colors met at its top and spread outward towards the earth. The lights shifted and danced with abandon.

 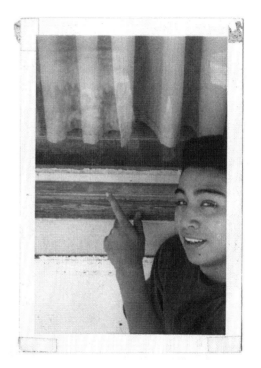

Omar was shot in the face, October of 1999. He is now dead.

Sept. 12, Fort Stockton, Texas

The water plunges and rises, whipped into foam. Steam floats around the brown and white fleshed people. They have given me money; a roach goes around the circle. For now we are contained by the thin aluminum walls of the shed. These walls lean into the sides of the whirlpool. Teresa's soft white skin gives to the touch—gives until you can press no harder, like, I imagine, the sheath of blubber insulating a seal. She pulls down her bikini top, showing the tops of her breasts which hang in long droopy tubes above her outstretched finger. It says, 'Maria,' there, tattooed in shaky italics and encased within a pale green-yellow pimiento. What's that, bitch, says one of the friends, his pointy head shaved clean, 7-2-5 U-S-M-C 0-0-9 inked along the top of his own breast like the collar to a cape. It's my daughter, she says, explaining. There was nothing I could do, she says. I would have taken care of her, if they'd given me the chance. You're lucky Daddy's got her now, says the other. I did a red pepper because they are fiery, like she will be, Teresa says. Why's it green then, bitch? says the other laughing. He ran out of red. The red was all taken, she says.

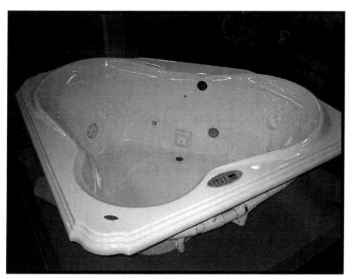

Later I would take my sister away from the mental hospital. We went to Niagara Falls. We parked at a casino on the Canadian side, next to a mess of tangled wires and tinted spotlights illuminating the sky. There was an old postcard in my sister's notebook: rowing near the edge of the falls, a superimposed cartoon drawing of two bears, with hearts floating in the air around them. 'I'm falling for you.' the caption read. The card was addressed to our mother. I had been with my father when he bought the card. He was not staying upstate, he was in a hotel only several miles away—he bought the card at a thrift store, he bought me an airplane made of balsa wood.

Sept. 14, Rt. 10 exit 159, Texas

Rt. 10 stretches forever across the state. It's a rancher now and a mute in the back—the truck smells of disinfectant, the grey velour seats pinstriped from the head of a vacuum cleaner. It's not good money, the rancher says. I won't lie. Hard work too, but room and board. We'll feed you, that's for sure. You're here at sundown, I'm coming back. Long before sundown, a gray coupe glides into the breakdown lane. Inside, the music beats in quick, reverberating swallows. There is a hairless hand on the gearshift with a gold chain that hangs lightly from the wrist. Then we are pulling over, too soon I think, for some drinks and then again just a few miles later. Next it's car trouble and he bends over the hood, watching me through the windshield . . . we pass two exits and once more leave the highway and climb up a ridge to a mud-choked pond. Got to let this engine cool off, he says. When he returns he's stripped down to his t-shirt and a thin pair of stained boxers, his legs sprawled out . . . I search the ground and begin picking rocks. I put three in my back pocket and throw one at the distant road sign. Look what I found, he calls. A dirty six-pack dangles from his arm with two empty plastic nooses. He watches me. I throw the second rock. All right, he says, let's get this going. But in the car we don't go. Look what I found. He flips through a magazine. Naked bodies. He flips pages and keeps flipping over and over the pages. Can you believe this, he says. He points and laughs at one picture. Then the car is moving again and the music thumping again, the magazine risen upon his lap. Sure is hot, he says, pulling over again now, peeling his T-shirt off over a smooth stomach. I twist the door handle, then am no longer in the car—running, the wrong way, but then thinking that there is no wrong way, not looking back, but still hearing the thumping, reverberating music. His car pulls in front of me, stops, the door opening. . . .

There are cracks in the country—in its families and highways, houses and rivers, factories, cellar windows, truck stops, in the sounds of chattering televisions, in the plexiglass booths of pay phones by bus stations, in the crushed glass of parking lots. . . .

Sept. 16, Las Cruces, New Mexico

In Las Cruces, off the exit ramp there is a sign for New Mexico State University. On the campus, bike paths peacefully snake between thick rugs of grass and beds of mulch planted with oaks. Endless empty parking lots. School is out, but there are some people. At the football stadium, cheerleaders practice. Their glossy tights shine amidst the overwhelming green astroturf like the sides of crashed spaceships. I've hidden my satchel under the bleachers. A campus guard tips his hat. His white teeth spread out, his chin points towards the cheerleaders. Early bird gets the worm, he says. Sprinklers dot the lawns, spraying mist around the transposed arcs of rainbows. In a dormitory building I find a shower. Downstairs, a TV lounge. Lucy and Ricky Ricardo dance and jostle across the screen and the tight confines of their apartment. Lucy's dog runs away and they spend days looking for it. The neighbors have it locked it up in their bathroom with a stack of steaks to keep it quiet. A young lady comes inside to say that the lounge is closing. She looks right through everything . . . as if I'm just a piece of furniture. It's a good feeling. I lie down to sleep in the space between some rhododendrons and a dormitory wall. I think of a letter I should write. I stare at the wall. I am listening to the sounds of music and late night conversations on the telephone—people laughing and breathing in each other's comfort.

I went to Mexico because of a scrap of paper that had an address scribbled on it. The address was supposed to be of a childhood friend, but I did not find him there. A girl picked me up in front of Cat's Paradox, a nightclub. I had snuck through the basement and fallen asleep underneath some coats in front of the cellar door. Her name is Eva Canalejo. Her father's name is Homero Canalejo, he is a famous writer. She showed

me his books. On the cover of one of them was a tattoo she had on the back of her neck. A portrait of their family by an artist named Red Grooms hung in their dining room. The mother felt sorry for me, she gave me a hundred dollars. The father opened the bathroom door and put a hand to his temple, I was brushing my teeth—he steered me out of the room and took a book out of his pocket. He tapped the book on my forehead and handed it to me, the book was Zorba the Greek by Nikos Kazantzakis. The entire family chain smoked Marlboros, they had a gentle German Shepherd. In fits of delusion I thought I saw the dog smoking sitting on an easy chair. I baked a huge chocolate chip cookie before I left, it was the only thing I had baked before, I used the recipe on the back of the package. I wrapped the cookie carefully in foil but when high on cocaine Eva ate it. The family left for New York and the maid came to me, she told me I could not go with them, she handed me a plane ticket to Matamoros.

Sept. 17, Albuquerque, New Mexico

My older son don't write me, but he's a good boy, she says. We park in a diner parking lot and tilt back the seats to sleep. When I wake in the morning, she's sewing shut the end of a pillow. A pocket with a tooth embroidered on it has been stitched in one corner. Here, she says. She opens her wallet and puts twenty dollars in the pocket and hands me the pillow. *This should be for your baby.* Oh, I can sew another one. Take it, I looked at your stuff. You got no pillow, this one's small, won't take up much space. You got a mother? *I'm trying to get back to my sister.* Well, it doesn't matter, but you should write somebody once you get someplace. I wish I could take you but I got my hands full, she says. In the back seat, the baby wails, a streak of sunlight across its tiny face. I don't want to take the money or the pillow. She shoos me out the car. In the parking lot, a black man with one gold earring and a pressed linen suit walks out of the diner. He looks me over, stops briefly and then waves his hand to get in his Escalade. I'm in real estate, he says. My wife's got another thing coming. The man has a CD player and plays Sade loud enough so we don't say anything. We pass the state line and he says, I got to go to the bank. You got any money? I'll make you a deal, he says, you pay for some gas now, then I'll run to the bank. I pay for some gas, he's still there, talking on his cellular phone. He puts one hand over the phone. Get me a sandwich, he says, I'll run to the bank. We'll make it to LA. Good things can happen to us in LA, he says. I reach into the pillow. He drives off to the strip mall down the street and his car disappears behind the bank. I wait at the station with the sandwich, he never comes back.

I worked at a toy factory, I worked at a restaurant washing dishes. People gave me money. I was ashamed, but I took the money, I never did not take the money.

Sept. 20, Boulder, Colorado

A man on a motorcycle with a Yorkshire terrier in the sidecar, a woman in a Volvo, and finally a water fountain, shade, a field of green grass. At a gas station, I see someone—a man I know. I run up to his van, but he doesn't remember me, until repeating my name twice, when he says he finally does. Hair make ninety percent of the man and you ain't got none anymore, Dave says. We start talking and smoke some reefer out of a wooden pipe shaped like a guitar. For the next three days, I stay in the van with him. We keep losing the keys until Dave ties them to his jeans with a piece of twine. There is half a copy of Moby Dick in a sleeping bag. The van is headed north soon. But then Dave disappears, he is not there anymore, his jeans are crumpled in the corner. The van is big, a twin mattress has been put on a frame in the back. Between the driver and passenger seats, the engine cover has been pushed back, the engine is exposed. A rubber glove sits on the dash to knock spark plugs back in place, it is fastened to the rear view mirror with another piece of twine. A wind-up radio fills the opened glove compartment. Tools, grease guns, flashlights, an old record player, a set of skis, spill out from around the bed frame. I wait for Dave, I look for him in town. No one knows him, he is gone.

My father was having an affair with another woman. He came downstairs to my room and she was there too, now sitting on his lap. "I wanted to show her your pictures," he said. She pointed at one on the wall: a man coming out of a cave was eating his own fist. "This is great," she said.

Sept. 26, Longmont, Colorado

The truckers back in against the dock bumpers and unload bundles of aluminum rods tied down together with tin straps. I snip the straps, jerk the rods onto a dolly and then wheel the dolly to the cutter on the other side of the factory. I slide the rods, five at a time, into the chute, the cutter revs until it sounds like an aircraft engine and the rods are snapped into smaller pieces. I use an asbestos glove to transfer the cut pieces to the metal press. Turning the crank by the side of the machine, with the rods pushed into the slots, the rods are bent into shape. It is my birthday. There is a clock and calendar on the wall. The van is parked in the back lot. Rigo comes and takes the rods from me. A retaining ring tightly fixes each plastic handle onto the aluminum slingshot frame. The factory makes slingshots, dumbbell handles and trash-cans with a basketball hoop on top. The workers butt the plastic end of the slingshot handle against their chests and lift the retaining ring on with their thumbs—their fingers are marked with a ridge of calluses and their t-shirts are dirty and worn through where they hold the handle against their ribs. Rigo duct-tapes pieces of cardboard inside his shirts to keep the cotton from wearing through. Rigo eats bologna and jalapeños for lunch, he brings me curtains to hang in the windows of the van. The bosses let me keep the car in the back and sleep in it as long as I power up the factory's machines in the morning. When I put a "For Sale" on the van, Rigo says he wishes he had enough money to buy it. At the end of the day, my last job is to crawl on the floor with a stick attached to a magnet. The magnet picks up balls of buckshot the company sells as slingshot ammunition—they spill all over the floor during the work-day. I'm under the plastic injector machine when I see a paint-splattered boot. Dave dangles the keys in front of my face. What the fuck? he says. It's my fucking van. Dave puts his boot on my stomach. I could, he says. He waves the boot in my face. C'mon, it's not starting, he says. Help me move the fucker. I collect my cash at the end of the week. The order is done, there's no more work.

When I was little I made things out of toothpicks: trains, cars, planes. I cut off the points and then glued the toothpicks together, sometimes I used popsicle sticks if I needed something bigger. Later I saved all the toothpaste tubes my family used and cut them open and cleaned them, I could fold and bend the metal into different shapes.

Sept. 28, Three Forks, Montana

Two roads meet like a cross upon the earth and there stops a middle aged man and his father and their truck. A dog squirms between them, its tongue dropping pearls of spit upon the upholstery. The younger man gets out, jerks his thumb to the bed of the truck where a sofa is lashed to the floor with heavy chains. The chains are spray-painted gold. The old man runs his liver-spotted hands through the dog's thick black fur, his eyes not leaving the windshield. You'll be king, he says. *Alright,* I answer. The younger man lowers the bed door, tests the chains. He's right, he says, you'll be king for now. King of the road.

There are places I kept returning to. At Craters of the Moon, I had a place to sleep that I was always able to find. Once I taped a drawing I found to the wall. When I came back several weeks later someone had written HELLO at the bottom of that piece of paper. They also left a tattoo gun made out of a toothbrush, a pen, guitar string and a tiny electric motor. I tried to use it but the batteries were dead. I had put a flower on the ceiling and they had put a second flower next to it.

Sept. 29, Colter Bay Village, Wyoming

Seven families, each with their own tent except for the grandparents who sleep in an RV. In the morning, the smell of pine needles, cooked bacon, four egg cartons and a milk jug full of pancake batter at the side of Grandfather. After breakfast is activity time. Then we swim out to the floating docks in the lake. Then tether-ball, drawing time. The children nap, the adults play scrabble. Grandmother stands up: time for a hike and nature lesson with Grandmother. Then the parking lot and the camp-store. Ham sandwiches. Grandmother becomes angry when she sees Grandfather drinking a Snapple. That's iced tea, Talmadge! she says. There's caffeine in that! You're setting a bad example, Talmadge! Talmadge throws out the bottle. Iced-tea is inseparable from summer, he says. My friend has gone to college, this year he does not come to the Mormon camp-out. He smokes cigarettes, Grandfather says, pointing at me. We're working on him and he doesn't count! Grandmother says. I am older than the other children, but not as old as any of the parents. Without my friend, the parents treat me gingerly—they are not sure how to act. I don't know how to act either, the children remember me, they drag me down to the lake to play. The grandparents have adopted an Indian woman with Down syndrome. When we play games, the families place us on opposing teams. Through her darkly tinted coke-bottle bottom glasses the Indian woman eyes me suspiciously.

Our apartment gets hot, the heater does not shut off in winter. You open the window before coming to bed. The morning chill permeates the air, incorporates itself into the fabric of space, stretches me, you, the walls, into a vast landscape. The corners of the room retreat. Then, you twist yourself into the sheets, your hair fanned against the pillow. You turn towards me.

Sept. 30, Moran Junction, Wyoming

The men have tattoos on their faces. Both have armor strapped to their shins. The larger one has a coat made out of feathers. Their hair is braided and the one without a coat has a plastic fuel-can strapped to his back. How you doing man? You got any water? *No.* You want a cigarette? Don't use the word cigarette fucker. It's a fucking corporate word. *Sure.* Feather-coat pulls out a pouch dangling from a necklace and rolls me a cigarette. We are standing by the camp-store. I have my duffel bag with me and a letter to mail. You going somewhere? *I'm going to try to get a ride, I think.* What the fuck are you doing? *This family is going back to Salt Lake—I'm not sure what to do.* Fuel-can man grabs the letter from me, his braids are tied into a chunky top-knot that whips around his head. You know the stamps have gone up, 37 fucking cents? You know what you got to do, you got to take the return address and reverse it with the real address. See, that way when they return the letter, they return it to where you want it to go. He pushes the letter back into my chest. We've got a camp, up in the mountains, he says. Hunting squirrels with slingshots and arrows and shit. But we're going to Riverton, heard there's some survival commune there, got a defensible retreat, got some bug-out kayaks right on the river. Feather-coat nods at me. I fold the letter and put it in my pocket.

After I left Rigo, Omar, Jose, the bearded man in the Volvo, Pinello, the man in the diner who put his food in a bag and put in on my lap, the woman who gave me a pillow: I always wanted to go back. Sometimes I ended up where we had met, but they were never where I had left them.

Oct. 1, Bondurant, Wyoming

Music and laughter can be heard from the road. In the woods is a clearing with a blazing fire, old men with furs. Lean Hispanic boys in jeans and fleece jackets sing Spanish songs to a white man playing a violin. More Hispanic boys lurk at the outskirts of the light, they seem happy, silent on their haunches. Twice a year we come down from the mountains, says one of the men. He passes me a jug filled with liquor. The Argentines bring down their sheep, we do some trading. A younger boy runs, jumps over the fire. *Do you live in a camp?* No, no, we trap, we go out on our own. The Indians work in teams of two. Some women will come up from town once the sun goes down. He laughs. They know what we're here for. *Are you survivalists?* No, he says, angry. Son, we've been doing this for hundreds of years, my dad lived on the Shoshone and his father the Gannett and his father before. Shit, every year someone asks me that. We like you townsfolk coming on up here, but we ain't museum pieces, he says. One of the boys begins playing an accordion and some of the men begin to dance. Three women appear from the woods. A police officer, in uniform, looks at the fire and takes the fire-jumper aside. Now the fire-jumper sullenly carves glyphs into the stump he sits on. The Argentines set up a table displaying bracelets, tablecloths and knitted rugs. The moonshine is not free anymore, several cars drive up and their lights push back the darkness. Skinned rabbits dangling from a pole are put over the fire. In the woods, a ragged line of inert bodies and patches of vomit stretches across the forest floor. Men put their hands on the trees to steady themselves while they piss. Smoke rises through the moonlight.

I went to the only friend I had. His parents were Mormon. With his family and other families we drove across the country in a caravan of mini-vans. We camped near the Teton Mountains. There was a three-legged race. I won a medal, printed on the tin, "favorite stranger: favorite new family member." Next year I got another medal, "Best loved hitch-hiker." One of the men worked in vice for the Salt Lake City police. At night he drank beer and I smoked cigarettes and his daughter plucked away at a plastic guitar while she sat on a log away from the fire.

Oct. 2, Robinson Butte, Wyoming

They come down the mountainside in an avalanche of dust, the men behind them, the dogs running at their sides, the ground unsteady. A labyrinth of wooden railroad tie fences pen them in, funnel them into a single file. A line of trucks sit ready. The men start a generator, fold the tents, whistle to the dogs. The sheep are silent, brooding. Those that have escaped do not go far, they hang their heads on the railroad ties.

We stayed high in the mountains, in a stone house. The men went out to get their things, they left me behind with the women and children.

Oct. 3, Pass Peak, Wyoming

The children make rope bracelets, the women watch them over their needlework. The oldest child sings a litany, a chorus of directions: Mano, mano. Dedo, pulgar. Gira. Mano, mano. This repeats, endlessly, softly, the only light from a flashlight propped in the corner, the children all weaving in unison. There are thousands of bracelets and embroidered tablecloths piled into garbage bags. Each time a bag is close to full, a boy brings it over to a rusted scale and weighs it. He then stands over me and watches me make a mark in their notebook. This is the job I have been given. Then the sound of trucks, one bright square of light marking the existence of a window. The men arrive, pushing back the canvas that serves as a door, crowding into the room with their ropes, their denim stained with sweat and dirt. Laughing, joking with the children, they haul the garbage bags into the trucks, lifting the children by their armpits into the flatbed, everyone now laughing, joking.

You wore a white dress. It was wet from the river, it clung to your body. I hid behind the rocks. The wire around my wrists had torn the fabric. What did you say? We swam, the water was cold. This should not be fading, is that what you said? What were you speaking about? This house is still here, the places are still here, trapped in photographs, the dress, our things, still there, unused and dusty in half-opened boxes.

Oct. 4, Signal Hill, Wyoming

The clouds have grown close. The sky turned from black to gray. I walk down the mountain, alone. The sounds of trucks and children and laughter has receded. The forest floor is soft, in a state of decomposition. An owl circles overhead. The pines end in shrubs, I push my way through them. Here, high on this mountain, several lines of bright white chairs stand on the grass in tidy rows. On a green field, two groups of chairs. Ten rows, seven chairs to a row. I sit. It begins to rain.

Please.

An abandoned rusted Bonneville. Upholstery hangs in tattered ribbons from the ceiling. The loud cracking report of a rifle. I slept, now I am awake, huddled on the floor at the foot of the front-seat. Two guns fire now, then three, a bullet puts a neat hole through the far back window. I can't speak loud enough (is this all a dream?) and time has collapsed: every movement I make slow and particulate. I reach forward and nudge my duffel bag out the opened rear door. Voices. Another gunshot. The gunshots stop. An outstretched hand pulls me out. Three boys, my age. Farking Christ, says one. Outside in the daylight, a jumble of trash: washing machines, shopping carts, condom wrappers, stuffed animals, shotgun shells on the ground. The boys bring me to a house. One of the boys pulls out a canister of bianca and the boys take turns seeing how many huffs they can take from it. They set up a wooden ramp on the driveway and skateboard in circles. Inside, we go down into a basement and they play video games. Stupid fucking controller, says one. Maybe I should come with you, says another. The mother comes down the stairs balancing a tray of lemonade on her arm. Then she goes away and returns with sandwiches. Who's this? she says. A friend of Jasper's, says a boy. You getting enough lemonade? she says, tugs down her apron. The couches in the basement are as long as cars. There's a phone on the end table. Some girls are meeting the boys down by the reservoir, by the dilapidated Bonneville.

When my friend picked up the phone, he told me to come home. I tried, many times, but I was always turned around.

Oct. 9, Portland, Oregon

One yells in English and the other in French. Someone has spray-painted the word "GODOGODJESUS" in two-foot high letters between the boiler pipes. I stand in the hallway and try to understand what either is saying until the sound of a TV drowns out their voices. At the end of the stairs is a small ceiling trapdoor. I pull myself through to the roof. A breeze drifts through the warm air. I use my blanket as a pillow. Pictures float on the backs of my eyelids: a long line of people stretches out in front of me. They are far away. The line curves over the horizon. I fly. I soar above the rooftops. On top of this building where I am flying is a tiki bar littered with cigarette butts and rolling papers. A stucco outhouse sticks up from the roof, it is half-filled with cages for pigeons, the other half with plastic planters and six-foot high stalks of marijuana under grow lights. The skinny man yelling in English says he is Portuguese, he walks without shirt or pants. I have not yet seen him wear anything other than tight, once white underwear. He has an Italian name, Pinello. He says an old woman left him the house because she liked his artwork. On the roof are piles of rocks, he says, for throwing at police. Pinello says the woman who gave him the house now lives in a mental institution and that the husband wants the house back. I hear more voices downstairs. On the street, I see two people I recognize: Feather-coat and Fuel-can man. I have been sleeping in the outhouse with the pigeons, I do not want these two men to come in the house, there is no room for them. Pinello will put them on the roof. I see Feather-coat rolling a cigarette and handing it towards the doorway. Pinello's girlfriend has stepped outside with him and draped a towel on his shoulders. He looks like a swimmer. Fuel-can man laughs, mimes putting some of his armor on Pinello's groin. Welcome to Casa de Los Gatos, Pinello says.

I told lots of people that I was going to find my sister. There were lots of places I invented, places where she supposedly lived.

Oct. 12, Portland, Oregon

He fables not; I hear the enemy. I don't understand, I say. We have to leave, Pinello says. Pinello pokes me in the shoulder, jumps off the bed. He piles bottles of liquor, motor-oil, maps into a wooden crate. I go outside onto the roof. Now I can hear a knocking on the door downstairs. Feather-coat man stands on the parapet. He looks at me, then Pinello. *Don't.* He drops his backpack, he jumps off the roof. He lies crumpled on the street, one arm bent oddly backwards. Now the flutter of real wings, the pigeons take to the sky. Fuel-can man emerges from the outhouse, Pinello takes a wine bottle and smashes it into his face. You don't burn it faggot, he says. The first lick of flame shoots out from the shed. Fuel-can man has lit the marijuana on fire. Pinello hooks a hand in his underwear and groans. Now, he says, that these idiots have ruined everything, we will have to make our escape through the back door. We leave Fuel-can man on the roof.

Abandoned, choked with weeds, plastic bottles, a wedding high in the mountains. Eva wrote me a postcard, it was pressed into the Pequod's yellowed pages, but now it is gone, slipped away.

Oct. 13, Lincoln City, Oregon

A parking lot by the sea, an ashtray on the dashboard. Windows cracked open, the sound of cars, music playing from a boombox. I wake because the driver opens the passenger door. He puts his hands on the hood, lights a cigarette and smokes. Then he goes down the steps, faces the seawall, kneels and prays. It is early morning, nothing but gray and fog. A chill comes through the open window. I thought that seeing the ocean would be the end of something. It is not.

In McCaren, Texas, I put my bag under the bridge, I took off all my clothes, the river was warm and slowly pulled me downstream. The lights of the town flickered through the leaves, dim gold spangles on the water. I felt clean, new. There was only me and you, everyone else was put away. Early in the morning I was awoken by the flashing lights of two police cars. They took a look at my driver's license, they asked me if I would be gone in the morning. They left me alone.

There are many things I have to tell you. I'd like to do that without speaking.

Oct. 14, La Pine, Oregon

The earth is wrong. The birds are gone or silent. The road broken. I sit in the lupine and wait. The sun pasted like a white disk in the sky. The dog has been following me, she squats just out of reach. I call the dog Betsy. Betsy and I are hungry. The pavement has ceased to function. What is this place? Betsy does not know. She is blameless. Silently we consider the steam pouring out of the earth.

I've lost pieces of things that I want to remember.

Oct. 15, Deschutes, Oregon

Shuffling through the leaves, holding myself upright by clinging to branches, I maneuver down the hollow, step onto a fallen tree trunk and walk along the horizontal trunk and onto a roof. A hole has been blown through the shingles. Down below, an overturned refrigerator and a girl sleeping inside of it. A green, wool blanket covers all of her except her hair, fanned out over the icebox. I climb down. The wooden floors of the house creak, an ironing board stands in the corner. But there is a hole in the roof, the whole house tilted down the slope, and a clock shaped like a cat with a tail still twitching the seconds. In the morning, the girl is gone.

The prairie was my cellar door.
I had removed everyone I knew
or the people had removed
themselves. I replaced them
all with a vast plateau, then
mountains, dry desert, broken
pieces of landscape that didn't
quite fit together. I found
people in the cracks.

Oct. 16, Ogden, Utah

Chickens scratch at the dirt road, a peacock stands motionless, one eye fixed in my direction. I wait for the car to pull out the driveway. Through the windows I see a litter box, couches, a framed diploma wedged between books. I wait for the car to come back. We sleep behind a eucalyptus tree. I wait for the car to leave again the next morning. Betsy whines as I tuck her into my arms. She licks the salt off my face. She squirms as I fill a bowl of water. I clear a space on the bottom of the coop. I put her inside. I walk away. She is crying.

Sometimes I wrote things down, fragments. But then I looked at them and they did not seem real and there seemed to be no purpose in writing them. There was nothing in them, other than things I did not want to remember.

Oct. 25, McCaren, Texas

A husband doesn't help if he isn't there. You're too young to understand. If he's good with his hands he won't cook or clean. I used to go places, we went places together. We didn't have any money in the beginning. Tabasco and toast, that's what we ate. Holly and I sit together in the movie theater. She leans into my shoulder. She puts her hand on my knee. When the lights come on, we go to the restaurant where she works. I sit at the corner table in the sun. At the end of her shift, Holly hurries out to her car. I see her open the door, sit down, start the car. Then she rolls down the window, gets back out and walks to my table. She wears sunglasses now. I'm sorry, she says, I can't take you home, I thought I might. She gets back in the car and the car reverses out to the highway. She is gone. An hour later, her white Jeep pulls into the breakdown lane. My wife told me you'd be here. A man gives me a hand into the car. She give you an earful? *Not really.* That's worse, the man says. He hands me a burger wrapped in butcher paper. He hands me a road atlas, a disposable camera, a tube of pepper spray. He picks the atlas off my lap and leafs through it. Boy, this is no place to be anymore. I was out there, far gone, when I was your age, then met her. We ain't going to last, but maybe we will. He puts the car in gear. He says, We both probably been thinking that so long that it doesn't matter. *It doesn't matter?* No.

I faded, subsumed by broken pieces of Americans and places—people, places and feelings all stitched together, larger than themselves, than me and you, all stretched around us, our life together, around the country.

This is how it began, in the middle. With no beginning. A bridge and a river.

Oct. 26, Gruver, Texas

The rear tires shiver free from the street momentarily and then shake themselves back in line. Then, tiresome, the car stops, the blue mustached officer stumbles bear-like into form from his hatch, screaming and beating his hood with his fists. And, I'm in the mud, no longer in the road, but he still screams, takes my knife, no good for anything other than rabbits. A momentary hallucination passes across my vision: a small marble balances on the police officer's forehead, the marble is aquamarine and brown. The police office stops screaming, stops speaking entirely. He drives off the highway with me in the backseat. We drive for several hours. I ask him where we are going. He doesn't respond. We drive farther. We drive over a truss bridge that bridges nothing. He lets me out on a dirt road. He comes from behind me and beats my face into the roof of his car. Then he kicks at the backs of my knees. I sleep that night in a cornfield.

We drove to the ocean and stopped the car in a field of bunchgrass and bluestem flowers. A white fence wound its way over the dunes. We stood in the sea and watched a line of boats going back to harbor. Our feet sunk into the soft sand. A row of sandpipers stuttered up the shore.

We did not speak.

Oct. 27, Boise City, Oklahoma

A laundromat with a television and bathroom . . . a man with a mustache and tight jeans, a pay-phone in the corner. Under the insole of my shoe are three dollars. I use the change machine and put quarters in the phone. No answer. My phone numbers have all gone old, everyone is moving, everyone is gone. I stare at one number a long time. I begin to leave a message. The man puts his hand on my shoulder—I am angry, he goes away. I get through to the mother of my friend, but I am not sure what to say, I hang up. I call Omar, I call Rigo. *What am I doing?* The operator asks for more quarters. The man swings himself up onto a drier.

At first, I lied to you.

Oct. 29, Denver, Colorado

Lee. Don't touch nothing. This is breaking my heart. Nobody knows nothing anymore. Nobody does anything, either. What you got in the bag? Lee throws a can out the window. Got to put all this together now. So bent, I'm fucking compressed, man. I'm putting it together. So compressed I'm losing things. Putting it all together. Everything she said. It's like a pill I've swallowed. I call her, I push myself into the phone. A little fucking ball rolling through the wires. *Who are you calling?* All pulled apart, losing things, losing quarters, losing—where we going, you tell me. *Denver.* Okay, Denver's good, straight roads, cold, Elway, got phones there.

Boxes piled in the backseat. The dash a tangled explosion of red and green wires. He carried an address book and a ziplock bag full of quarters in his lap. We stop at payphones, we avoid eye contact. We looked at each other only once.

Nov. 1, Walden, Colorado

Patches of snow cover the ground, but it is not cold. It is night—a blue-black pincushion sky, dense with stars. Inside the helicopter a candle flickers, illuminating the shape of a man in a sleeping bag, an oriental rug, bottles of water and stacks of canned cat food. A map is taped to the wall, lines have been drawn from spots on the map to the margins, each line ending in a crowded scrawl of letters and numbers, coordinates and temperatures, illegible words. I wonder how long he has been out here.

I was underneath a park bench. This woman, a girl really, kept approaching me. I had read Nikos Kazantzakis. I tried to talk to her about this, but she did not know who that was. But she knew a brother named Nikos and for some reason she was looking for him under a park bench. She would not help me, but she seemed like an angel: an angel in picture books, she was not like you, she was distant and involved in something I did not understand.

Nov. 2, Rawlins, Wyoming

Where's Nikos? Where's Nikos? shouts an angel. There is a white dress, a ribbon, a worried floating face. I move my hand out from under the park bench, *Here, Here* . . . I whisper, *Here I am!* She pats my head, crosses my wrists urgently. No, No, she says, Not you. Let's find Nikos, she says. *Please! Take me with you!* No, No, she says again, you can't stay here or with us. It's Nikos I'm looking for, not you. You are nobody.

I am losing these pieces, they just fall away and clatter along behind me. I am making a scene. Here in the grocery aisle, at the bus station, in the parking lot. Even here, when I want things to come out the best way they can.

Nov. 4, Craters of the Moon National Park, Idaho

The earth is black and buckled. Dunes of rock squeeze out of the ground like toothpaste that has dried and become cracked and fissured. Someone has drawn an arrow in chalk marking the way back to the road. A large bird glides through the sky. The land is vast and barren. When a car passes on the edge of the distant horizon it appears only as a speck of white light. Here, in the middle of nothing, is a rusted bronze plaque: Incinerated Forest (Tree Molds). Taped to the plaque is a purple flower and a piece of paper. I pick up the paper and put the tape and flower in my pocket. A boy with a crown sitting on a rock orbiting the earth is drawn on the paper. Written underneath the drawing are the words, "What makes the desert beautiful, says the little prince, is that somewhere it hides a well." Past the plaque is a field pockmarked with deep holes, each half-filled with iridescent oil-slicked water. Past that is a hump of sagebrush, past that a mound of broken boulders. In between two large stones is a shallow cave I lay down in. I tape the drawing and words to the side of the cave and push the flower into a small map of lichen on the ceiling.

It's gone, he said. You can't get it that way.

Nov. 6, US Atomic Energy Commission Reservation, Arco, Idaho

The road is a tight, thin line. No shoulder, each side guarded with loops of barbed wire and electric fencing: metal signs with skulls and crossbones threaded into the electric wires every few feet. An SUV stops in the middle of the road, the door opens, the car belches a fog of cold air. The man puts forth his hand and shakes mine, tightly bunching my knuckles together. He is past middle-age, with creased khakis, tinted glasses and a flattop haircut. I look at everything as an opportunity, he says. I'm a Toastmaster, do you know what that is? You an army kid? *My father was in the army. . . .* Well, he says, I'm Marines. He rests his right hand behind my headrest. See, I can talk about anything—it's about communication. Just give me a topic. Okay, let's just look out the window, he says. What's out there, looks like nothing. Looks like a wasteland, right? I look out the window. But there is no nothing, he says. He moves his driving hand to gesture at the land outside. This is a large caldera, covering thousands of square miles. An area of pressure building up. All this empty nothing was dumped here thousands of years ago, heaved out from the earth itself, tons of rock and ash. All life for hundreds of miles extinguished instantly—a black cloud from Mexico to the Mississippi. Now those aren't just rocks that you're looking at. *Not just rocks,* I say. That's right, he says. Now let's go one step forward, let's deepen the discussion. See them signs, those smokestacks in the middle of nothing? *Yes.* That's man. Man's put his hand in the pie, that's nuclear power. Now let's really get out there. What do you think about nuclear power? *I don't know.* Okay, well. The Russians blew a 100 kiloton bomb, out in the Arctic Sea in 1948. Nova Zembla. That's nothing compared to what happens if this caldera goes again.

And it'll happen again, bet your pants—but, here's the kicker, it probably won't for a hell of a long while, that's in the science fiction future. But what we got here, we got atomic energy in the middle of nowhere, with fissile material just coming in and out every day. This is today, this isn't fiction. *Okay.* Hold on, I'm really humming now. So you got fissile material, a gram of which makes a little backpack nuke and you got it sitting on top an area of massive geothermal pressure. Do the math, can you see where I'm going? It could be anti-government people, could be an inside job, could be some Russians still on the inside, could be the Belgians, no one suspects them, could be anybody. Oh yeah, lot a people got their eye on this spot of nothing.

When you are on the side of the road, when you are on a train, you are not free, it is the opposite of freedom. You are a vessel for the world to fill, or throw against the wall, God turns the radio dial of your life. The Mormons expected me every year, where else would I go? They were always there.

Nov. 9, Lemmon, North Dakota

The officer smiles. We'll put you up in a hotel if you got no place to stay. Then get you on your way tomorrow. The dog's nose sticks out the window, it looks familiar, a German Shepherd. Moxie! Outside! I can hear the mechanical whir of the window as Moxie somehow opens the window. She jumps out. The dog runs to me and sits quietly at my feet. She paws at my thigh and then nibbles at my jeans' pocket. Oh boy, well you'll be staying in my hotel now, says the officer. He pushes the dog's snout away and picks through my pockets. At the station, he shows me a wall of cork-board filled with pipes, chore boy sponges, and syringes. He walks me into a barred room painted beige. A cube cage sits in the middle of the room and he puts me in it, there are four bunk beds and nobody in any of them except me. He takes out some nails and spray-glue and carefully mounts what I had onto the board in the hallway. He writes on a label and affixes the label underneath. Then he lets me out and we walk outside to the gas station on the corner. He hands me the notebook at the bottom of my duffel bag and points at the payphone. You got twelve dollars, he says. You need 200, if you don't want to sleep in the big house tonight. Cars start appearing in the lot. The policeman stands behind me, he hands me some quarters. The men haul themselves out of their cars and lean on their hoods smoking cigarettes. Boy, this is a friendly community, the officer says. I stare at the phone numbers in my book. The first two won't go through. One number is in Mexico and I don't have enough quarters. Another, someone picks up the phone and has no idea who I'm asking for. I get through to the factory and ask for Rigo. Rigo says he'll wire me fifty dollars. More people arrive. Another dial-tone, an answering machine. I don't want anyone to pick up now—I just want to be moving again. I'm out of quarters. You can work it off, says the officer, Three, four days. He puts a hand on my back and the crowd parts as he pushes me back to the station.

When people are gone
there is nothing you can
say to them. Most of these
people are gone, the places
too: they are paved over,
removed, relocated, trans-
formed. The tenses are lost,
misplaced, the difference
between subject and object
are confused. I myself am
confused, misplaced, gone.

Nov. 12, Bismarck, North Dakota

The men all have names: Red, Sparta, Old Sam, Pretty Boy, V.A., Big 'Un. We pick up trash by the interstate. We wear bright orange vests that have to be on us at all times. It isn't that different from standing by the side of the road by yourself. A van picks us up and brings us to a park, a forest ranger shows the guard where we should begin to make trail. Red, Pretty Boy and I do the clearing, Sparta, VA, and Rescue, the tilling. Old Sam cleans up the brush that we leave behind and then Big 'Un comes up from the back to tamp the trail flat. The fire rake I have is like a fork with stubby teeth. Laboring silently, we end up in groups of two or three strung out along the trail. Larry is my god-given name, Big 'Un tells me—his one lazy eye sliding off towards the sky. A vine unfolds to touch my shoulder and I turn around, expecting to see the guard. Instead, the hissy spit of frightened deer comes from a copse of locust trees back in the woods. I crouch down to one knee and look for them through the branches. Everywhere brown leaves shift against the flanks of gray trees. You know you done after today? says Big 'Un. You going to eat your lunch?

When I was in prison, every night they would bring in the same woman. She vomited on the floor between our beds. I know that she was very upset about something and that one day when they walked her in, she jumped out in the street and tried to fall in front of the car passing by. I remember thinking that it was strange, because if someone was making a movie of her, the movie would not be good. She was a bad actress, but there was no movie, there was no acting. I remember she asked me if she could have my jeans so she could hang herself. I remember sitting up and talking to her and listening to her talk to herself but I cannot remember a single word of what she talked about. I cannot remember what she looked like. I cannot remember her name.

Nov. 14, Pueblo, Colorado

The brakeman stumbles then points to a sign, the gravel snickering under his boots. He lurches forward in warning and then abruptly twirls and shoots one hand forward beckoning me onward, past a mottled, incongruous poodle and through a frail, rusted fence of barbed wire. The dog slithers on its belly and quickly disappears, under the splintering grey shack of leaning wood planks, the man shouting as he kicks the door jamb, Git Bessie, Git on outta under there, he says. Inside, a stove littered with pots, pans, then a match lit to blue-flame, hissing water. You ain't gonna git it that way, says the man, tugging at my sleeve and with a stick scraping the inside of one dusty window. It ain't out there, he says. It ain't out there, he says, it's gone. . . .

I wanted to be with you, or not to be there at all. I called many times. I couldn't find you. You weren't there yet. So, I chose not to be there. But I was unable to do even that. They replaced the strings on my wrists with a blue hospital band.

I walked alone to the bus station.

Nov. 16, Grand Junction, Colorado

The grass and gravel move along—shut the door. Rain whipping on through the half-open boxcar. The door stuck. A garbage bag in one corner already filled with human waste. The sounds of rushing air, groaning iron. The deafening sounds. Moon. Juniper.

Jose was fired from Atlas VanLines. He went back to Mexico and works on a tour bus with his nephew.

When we met there was you and me and me and Jose and Bessie and me and Rigo and Omar and Tom and Maria and a little girl with no shoes on. There were so many shells of myself that I could not put them together. I just left them where they stood.

Nov. 18, Rifle, Colorado

We fucking really got him, says one of them. Fuckin A, says another, pounding the steering wheel. Bitch fucker! Three shining moons jab at the air, rocking with laughter. The car is bouncing and I am sweating. They are not talking about me; I do not know what they are talking about. I look down at my hands and see I have dropped my drugs on the floor. The third one slaps the headrest. There is more excitement and their heads jab back and forth again. It is getting hot and the air reeks of sweat. I search on the floor amidst the beer cans and road maps but my head is beginning to swim. There is a body slumped next to me on the seat. The vinyl is sticky with blood. Who is this body? I try to spread out some of the trash, probing now with my foot, but I can't reach. Resting my forehead against the cool windowpane—my eyes close. They are closed.

We were going to move in together, you put my things in the car. We drove away. At the bottom of my duffel bag you found a wooden toolbox my mother had given me. Inside was a small leather wallet, some curled guitar strings, a coffee mug from a rehabilitation center, a smudged drawing of a boy standing on the moon, a handmade medallion, a boxcar made out of toothpicks, a water-stained comic book, a piece of glass with a leaf carved in it, a dried flower, a slingshot, a child's pillow, a folded letter

with a 35-cent stamp, a stack of photographs. You put some of these things on the mantel. When you went to work, I put them away, into cardboard boxes. Later, I told you that I threw them out.

Nov. 20, Vernal, Utah

There are pictures on the mantle. The girl is not in any of them. She twists paperclips into her hair, puts water on to boil. Who's this? The boyfriend turns on the TV, turns it off. In the basement we find a linen closet and, inside, blankets to bring up. Lincoln logs and miniature cowboys and indians are spread along the carpet. *Do you know who these people are?* No. The three of us sleep by the back door.

You go to work, I walk into the kitchen. I start the coffee. I look at the clock and begin to wait.

Nov. 22, Fort Collins, Colorado

You know this song, you gotta serve somebody? The man moves slowly, he has a scraggly beard going grey; he reaches over and turns up the volume on the cassette player. I'm not so sure about it, he says. Silence, time passes, the needle on the car's fuel gage falls through ¾, to a ½ ,to a ¼. The fuel light turns red. We pull in to a gas station. At three in the morning, he suddenly says, You remind me of someone, he didn't say anything to me either. We stop at a supermarket and the man goes out and brings back some apples, peanut butter, and crackers. Hours later, when we stop for gas a second time, he begins talking again: He was rangy like you, he had hazel eyes. He set this little old bird down in A Shau and he got me out of there, I didn't deserve to get out, it wouldn't mattered one bit to me if I was still there lying in the bush. I don't think the outcome of anything mattered to either of us at that time—he could of died, I could of died. But somehow it matters to me now. It matters if I think of the wife and kids I got, it matters to me that he had those little ropes of kite-string tied to his wrists and he was strong enough to pull me out with one hand without me helping much. And I just don't see any connection between that *me* lying there hot and itching and fading away, and the *me* now, but sure was he able to patch me up in that chopper. Something about your eyes and that you have these guitar string tied on your wrists, and the way you're not even looking at me but you're here all the same whether you know it or not, something about that reminds me of you or him—I don't know it all gets jumbled together. . . .

I began this story before the story in Dubois. The bottle I stole was from the restaurant where I worked washing dishes. These bales of hay are behind the Forest Service's worker trailers. I had once rented a room in one of the trailers. When I returned I knew nobody. But it was still the closest thing to a home I had. The ranger occupying the trailer had no idea who I was, but I convinced him to let me stay outside. I demonstrated knowledge of the town and of his living quarters enough to convince him. But I could not stay very long, the little home that I had had moved along without me.

Nov. 23, Dubois, Wyoming

A shirt, rolled into a u-shape, makes a pillow. Beyond, there is the trailer where I stayed last night and, next to it, the lot of dust and grass and three more homes neatly parallel. Above them, a concrete dike holds back the leveled hill where are the muddy pasture, the barn, and the hay bales atop which I sometimes sleep. The horses below snort, whinny, twitch their hooves. From here I can see the lines of their skulls and the dark elliptical rocks of their eyes. A trio of mules nestle their shorter heads against the splintered grey wood of the corral and past them, around the bend, and two streets down, into town behind the service station, is where the bottle I took came from. Below my body, giant towers of hay sway like the roofs of houses in a flood.

It's all about to be swept away again.

There was nowhere to go, as long as I was myself.

Nov. 25, Cheyenne, Wyoming

There is a stool to sit on and a thin, clear tube that winds its way from open lips to across the table into a box. Breathe, says the man holding the box. He jots something down in the notebook propped against his forearm. Then he looks up and a list of questions follow. Are you sick? How long will you stay? Do you have a birthmark? Tattoos? Cigarettes? Do you understand? He searches the face in front of him for an instant and then waves me off. At nine o'clock he blows a whistle and is replaced by a chaplain. There is TV and then out come styrofoam bowls of rice hiding rosy disks of sliced hot dog. At ten it's the showers and second-hand hotel robes are handed out, warm from being left on the heaters. Four at a time everyone is herded into the locker room. An older man hums and another ducks under the arc of steamy water. Quarter to eleven the whistle sounds again and a closet full of mattresses is opened. There is some discussion, some fighting. Then the lights go out and it's time for sleep. Someone whispers about my bedroll, my jacket. I tie everything in a bundle and strap it to my arm. Darkness. The whistle blows again. A line forms to put the mattresses in the sanitizer bin. Breakfast is cereal. A new man at the counter unlocks a drawer and doles out some cigarettes, then opens the door, yawning as the men file out. The crisp air comes down from the mountains, blows down off the butte and rushes down the exit ramp.

I always wanted to write you a letter from back then. I'm sorry it's all in pieces.

This is how it was with me.

This is that letter.

Acknowledgments

Excerpts from this novel appeared in *Sleepingfish* and *H.O.W.* (Helping Orphans Worldwide). The author gratefully acknowledges those editors, Derek White and Alison Weaver, for their generosity.

The author would also like to thank Christian Janss, James Graves, John Donohue, Mark Pritchard and Evelyn Zornoza for allowing use of their photographs, Eric Ulrich for his advice—and Wilkes County Correctional and The National Park Service for their cooperation.

For their unwavering support, he would also like to thank Pablo, Jesus, Jeanne, Rafael and, most of all, Evelyn.

About the Author

Andrew Zornoza is a visual artist and writer born in Houston, Texas and now residing in Brooklyn. His fiction and essays have appeared in magazines such as *Sleepingfish, Confrontation, Porcupine Literary Arts, CapGun, Matter Magazine, Gastronomica* and *H.O.W.* He can be found teaching writing at The New School University and fiction at Gotham Writer's Workshop.

TARPAULIN SKY PRESS
Current & Forthcoming Titles

Jenny Boully, *[one love affair]**

Ana Božičević, *Stars of the Night Commute*

Traci O Connor, *Recipes for Endangered Species*

Mark Cunningham, *Body Language*

Peter Davis, *Poetry! Poetry! Poetry!*

Danielle Dutton, *Attempts at a Life*

Sandy Florian, *32 Pedals and 47 Stops*

Noah Eli Gordon & Joshua Marie Wilkinson, *Figures for a Darkroom Voice*

Adrian Lurssen, *Angola*

Gordon Massman, *The Essential Numbers 1991 - 2008*

Paul McCormick, *The Exotic Moods of Les Baxter*

Joyelle McSweeney, *Nylund, The Sarcographer*

Teresa K. Miller, *Forever No Lo*

Jeanne Morel, *That Crossing Is Not Automatic*

Andrew Michael Roberts, *Give Up*

Joanna Ruocco, *Man's Companions*

Brandon Shimoda, *The Inland Sea*

Kim Gek Lin Short, *The Bugging Watch & Other Exhibits*

Chad Sweeney, *A Mirror to Shatter the Hammer*

Shelly Taylor, *Black-Eyed Heifer*

Emily Toder, *Brushes With*

G.C. Waldrep, *One Way No Exit*

Max Winter, *The Pictures*

Andrew Zornoza, *Where I Stay*

&

Tarpaulin Sky Literary Journal
in print and online @

www.tarpaulinsky.com